CUPS HELD OUT

JUDITH L. ROTH

ILLUSTRATED BY BROOKE ROTHSHANK

*For Melody
a wonderful teacher —
May God bless you
so you may bless others
Love,
Judith L. Roth
2007*

Herald Press
Scottdale, Pennsylvania
Waterloo, Ontario

Library of Congress Cataloging-in-Publication Data
Roth, Judith L.
    Cups held out / Judith L. Roth ; illustrated by Brooke Rothshank.
        p. cm.
    Summary: A girl and her father drive from San Diego to Mexico, where they encounter poor children and beggars and they ponder their feelings of guilt and their responsibility to those who live in poverty.
    ISBN 0-8361-9316-4 (pbk. : alk. paper)
    [1. Poor—Fiction. 2. Poverty—Fiction. 3. Mexico—Fiction.] I. Rothshank, Brooke, ill. II. Title.
    PZ7.R72787Cu 2006
    [E]—dc22

                                    2006016224

We didn't get here on a cruise ship
like lots of these tourists.

We drove here from San Diego.

First through Tijuana,
  past plywood shacks,
  up a tall road
     to a view of the bull ring,
  crazy-driving around
     a confusing circle of roads.

Now we're in Ensenada.
Dad says it's safer here than Tijuana,
    and it's prettier,
    and it's more like the real Mexico.

He's ready this time.

Dad was here a long time ago
    and he wasn't ready then
        for the beggars.

He didn't expect
    sad-eyed women with babies tied on their backs
    and cups held out for money.

11

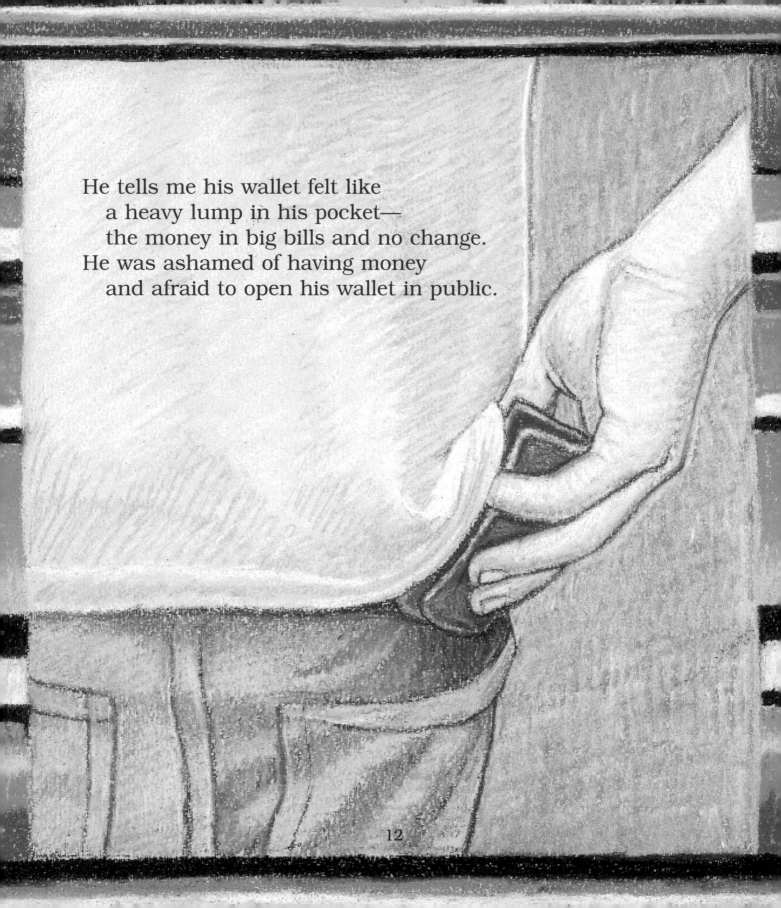

He tells me his wallet felt like
a heavy lump in his pocket—
the money in big bills and no change.
He was ashamed of having money
and afraid to open his wallet in public.

12

But now he is ready.
And I am ready.
We park by the beach
and look out at the water.

13

We walk past some statues,
   and I take a picture.

We walk up the side street
   that goes to the main market
      and Dad says,
"Let's look first, in here."

So we go into a shop
   crammed with stuff.

"See if there's anything
   you want to buy,
and then we'll go," Dad says.

So I look.

14

15

I would like the chicken piñata
    and a silver bracelet
and two brightly-painted pots
    for my plants at home.

Dad says he's bought a blanket
    every time he's come down here.
But we don't buy anything yet.

We go back on the street
    and head for the main
        shopping area.

17

And we start to see them.
A small group of kids
who go up to people
and ask for change.

18

Women with
their babies
sitting silently
on the sidewalk
holding their old
Styrofoam cups.

19

"This doesn't feel right, either,"
    says Dad.
But when the children
    come to us,
I give them a quarter
    from the stash
        deep in my pocket.

20

And into every raised cup,
Dad drops a dollar.
He has twenty-five bills
lined up in his pockets—
each dollar folded and ready.

One of the kids says,
   "Hey, you got some gum?"
`But I don't have any.
   And what I have seems dumb.

There is a little girl with sparkly eyes
   who smiles at me
   even though I've run out of quarters.

I wish I could know her.
But it's getting late,
   and the ready money is gone
   and Dad says we've seen enough new things
      to fill up our heads for a while.

We drift back to the first shop.

Dad says, "I think maybe it helps a poor country
    if you buy things there." He shrugs.
"It gets some more money into the country, at least."

27

So Dad picks out a blanket
   and I pick out a chicken piñata
and we carry them back to the car.

28

29

We sit quietly in the car.
Dad doesn't start the engine.

He says he doesn't know what to do
    about the poor people.
But he wants me to know about them.

He wants me to know the poor are
    part of this world.
"Maybe next time," he says.
    "Maybe next time we'll. . . ."

And we both think about
    what we might do.

One thing I know:
   Back home, in a clean
      well-lit store,
   there's a shiny forest-green bike
      with hand brakes
      and a special water bottle.
   It costs $189.97.

It's the most beautiful thing I've ever seen.

32

But I think my old blue bike
is plenty enough for me
right now.

The Author

Judith L. Roth has been an editor and a youth minister. Her poetry has appeared in over a dozen magazines. She is a songwriter and a writer of biblical study books, but her first love is children's fiction. Besides writing curriculum, she is presently at work on several fiction books for different ages. This is her first picture book.

The Illustrator

Brooke Rothshank is a painter and illustrator who has an affinity for working in glass, portraiture, and art for children. Her works have been exhibited at the Chicago International Miniature Exhibit and the Andy Warhol Museum. She holds a bachelor's in painting from Goshen (Indiana) College.